BARNEY GOOSE

A Wild Atlantic Way Adventure

For Killian, Stella & Tommy - *CAT*

Carol Ann Treacy is an Irish children's author, illustrator and graphic designer. She lives in Kilkenny in a very messy house with her husband, two children and a bunch of wild cats; She loves to travel and sometimes wishes she could fly. She thinks geese are great. Honk!

Acknowledgements

I would like to thank all my family and friends for their continued support.
A special thanks to Laura Browning and my editor Eoin O'Brien of The O'Brien Press.

First published 2020 by The O'Brien Press Ltd,
12 Terenure Road East, Rathgar, Dublin 6, D06 HD27, Ireland
Tel: +353 1 4923333; Fax: +353 1 4922777
E-mail: books@obrien.ie
Website: www.obrien.ie
The O'Brien Press is a member of Publishing Ireland.

ISBN: 978-1-78849-142-6

6 5 4 3 2 1
22 21 20

Printed and bound in Drukarnia Skleniarz, Poland.
The paper used in this book is produced using pulp from managed forests.

Barney Goose receives financial assistance from the Arts Council

Published in

DUBLIN
UNESCO
City of Literature

BARNEY GOOSE

A Wild Atlantic Way Adventure

Written & Illustrated by

CAROL ANN TREACY

THE O'BRIEN PRESS
DUBLIN

Barney Goose started life as an egg. Tom the lighthouse keeper found him washed up on the beach in West Cork.

Tom took him home
and kept him warm
until he **hatched**

5

Barney Goose spent
the whole winter at the
lighthouse, following
Tom around.

6

Tom fed him all the things that geese love: leaves, roots and weeds. Yum! He was growing fast.

Barney loved living at the lighthouse. But when spring came, he felt that it was time to go, though he didn't know why.

Honk!

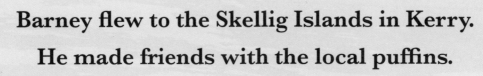

Barney flew to the Skellig Islands in Kerry.
He made friends with the local puffins.

They told him jokes, and rolled about laughing.
Then Barney looked up at the sky and felt it was
time to go, though he didn't know why.

Honk honk!

In Limerick some curious deer watched as Barney flew down into the forest to eat some supper.

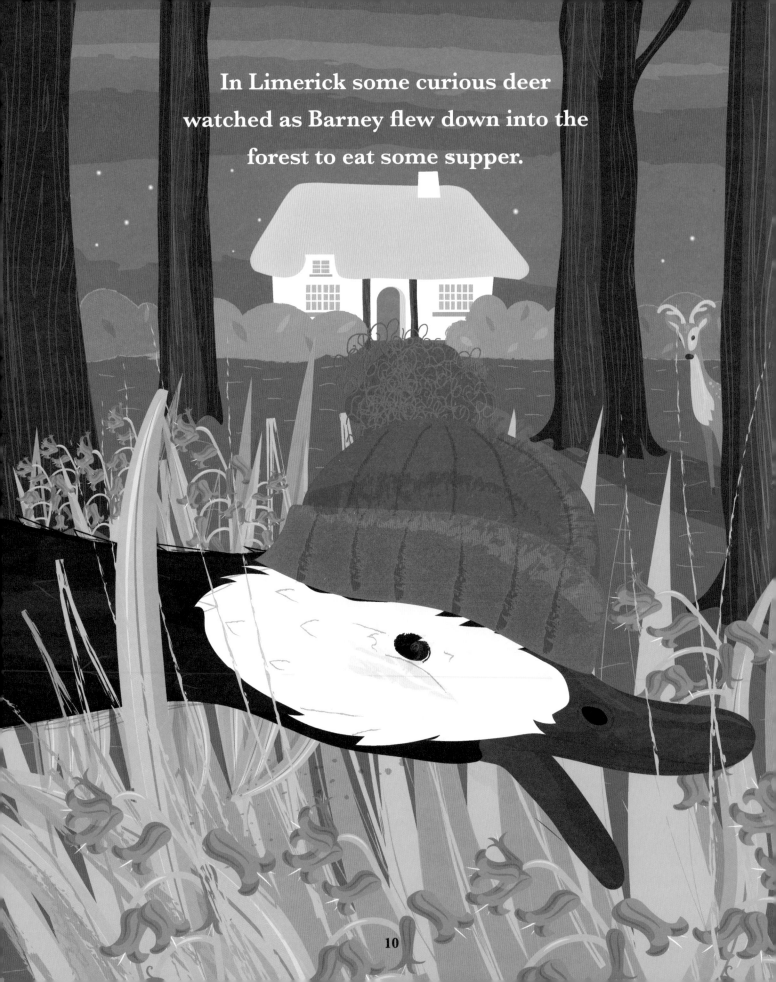

Then Barney knew it was time to go,
though he didn't know why.
Honk honk honk!

By early morning, Barney was hungry again. He landed in the Burren in Clare, and some friendly rabbits gave him crunchy carrots for breakfast.

Then Barney felt he really had to go, though he
didn't know why. The rabbits waved him off
as he disappeared over the Cliffs of Moher.

13

Barney spotted a group of friendly dolphins in Galway Bay.
He swooped down and they splashed around and played
games together all day ...

... until their mother called the dolphins away.
Barney was tired now. He tucked his head
beneath his fluffy wings and fell fast asleep.
Honk ... zzz ... honk ... zzz

The next morning Barney awoke with a jolt.

'You're drifting out to sea!'

boomed an enormous whale, as he squirted Barney

back towards the shore with a jet of water.

Barney flew on, and skidded down
on a beautiful lake in Mayo.

Three elegant swans watched and smiled as he tried some waterskiing. Then Barney knew he had to keep going, though he really didn't know why.

Honk honk honk honk!

As Barney flew over Sligo the waves were getting bigger. He waved to a family of seals stretched out on the rocks. His stomach fluttered as he flew – something inside was driving him on. He had to keep moving, though he still didn't know why.

Honk honk honk honk honk!

As he flew across Leitrim, a great storm arose.
The sea raged and the wind howled. Barney beat his wings
as he passed sheep huddling beneath Eagle's Rock.
He was getting very tired now. He was nearly ready to drop,
when an eagle swept down out of the clouds above.

'Follow me, little one, I will guide you through!'

said the eagle.

Honk honk honk honk honk honk!

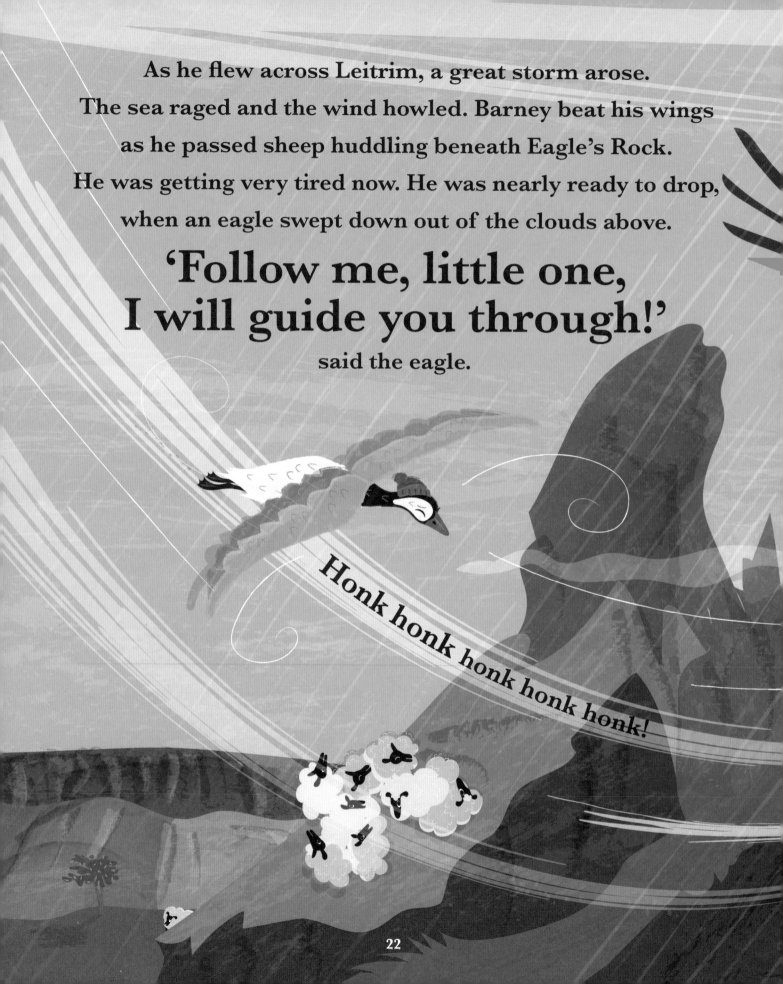

As Barney soared over the hills of Donegal the clouds
parted and the sun shone warmly on his back.
He could tell he was going the right way,
though he still didn't know why.
As he rounded Malin Head he heard a sound that
made his heart sing ...

Honk Honk Honk Honk Honk

Honk Honk Honk

Honk

It was a sea of honking geese,
just like him!

The geese were all migrating across the
Atlantic Ocean to Greenland,
like they did every summer.

As they flew off across the northern lights,
Barney had never felt so happy.

Honk!

30

Now Barney has lots of new friends
along the Wild Atlantic Way.
But he still comes back to visit Tom
at the lighthouse in west Cork every year.

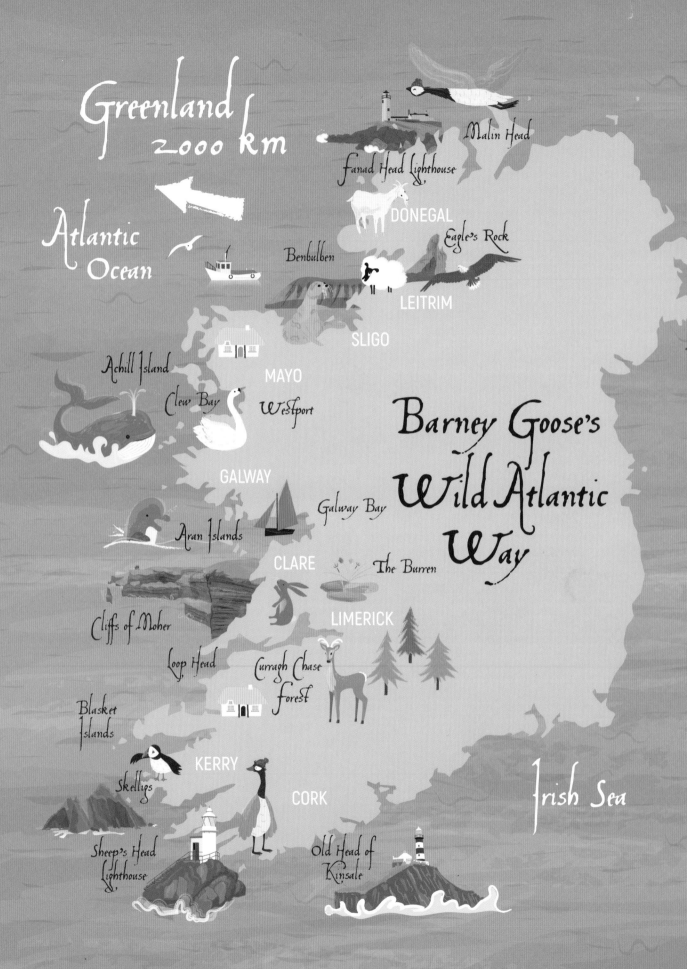

Greenland
2000 km

Atlantic
Ocean

Malin Head

Fanad Head Lighthouse

DONEGAL

Eagle's Rock

Benbulben

LEITRIM

SLIGO

Achill Island

MAYO

Clew Bay

Westport

GALWAY

Barney Goose's
Wild Atlantic
Way

Aran Islands

Galway Bay

CLARE

The Burren

Cliffs of Moher

LIMERICK

Loop Head

Curragh Chase
Forest

Blasket
Islands

KERRY

Skelligs

CORK

Sheep's Head
Lighthouse

Old Head of
Kinsale

Irish Sea